ELEPHANTS
HAVE RIGHT OF WAY

Sylvia Sherry

Illustrated by Quentin Blake

JONATHAN CAPE
London

First published 1995

1 3 5 7 9 10 8 6 4 2

Text © Sylvia Sherry 1995
Illustrations © Quentin Blake 1995

Sylvia Sherry and Quentin Blake 1995

First published in the United Kingdom in 1995 by
Jonathan Cape Limited
Random House, 20 Vauxhall Bridge Road, London SW1V 2SA

A CIP catalogue record for this book
is available from the British Library

ISBN 0 224 03670 X

Printed in Hong Kong

0224 036 70X 5518.

Contents

Chapter One

THE boy's head appeared round the edge of the open shed. His large dark eyes took in the heap of worn tyres, the bench with the tools carefully laid out, the drums of oil, the bottles of soft drink in the corner. Then his eyes moved to the old car in the centre of the shed. And then to the pair of dungareed legs stretching from under it.

The boy said nothing. Outside the shed, the sun beat down on his back. Inside the shed, his face was shadowed, his eyes gleaming in the dimness. He watched the legs.

Suddenly, there was a curse from under the car, the legs moved and the body wriggled from under the car and got to its feet – a short, stout body in oily dungarees with a turbanned head on top. The boy watched as the man threw a wrench down on the bench.

"My God, this is a bloody awful job!"

The man reached for a bottle of orange squash, prized off the cork and drank. He wiped a hand over his sweaty forehead, turned and saw the boy.

"What are you doing here, boy? I sacked you yesterday. Clear off!"

The boy's large, dark eyes watched him steadily.

"Mr Singh . . ."

Mr Singh stepped out of the garage. The sun threw his craggy face into deep lines. He pointed a long, oily forefinger at the boy.

"Did I sack you yesterday?"

The boy nodded.

"Did you do four hundred shillings worth of damage in one week? Six days only?"

The boy gestured with his hand. "These things that happened – "

"*Did* they happen? Did you drain the radiator of that Ford Cortina and send it out dry with its owner? Did you break that bloody new jack trying to lift that lorry?"

"It was not a new bloody jack, Mr Singh – "

"Did it happen? Did you spray paint all over the windscreen of that bloody Peugeot belonging to Mr Manani, chief clerk at Kabete stores?"

The boy's large dark eyes continued to regard him.

Mr Singh heaved a great sigh. He thrust his hands into his pockets and surveyed the street, the cars, the motor bikes, the mopeds, the Masai in a red blanket striding along the opposite pavement, the Kikuyu women with their bundles supported by straps across their fore-

heads on their way to market, the hawker trundling a barrow piled with second-hand furniture, the office workers, brisk in white shirts and dark trousers, the two cheeky kids in Sinatra type straw hats from the grocer's next door watching from the edge of the pavement.

"I am damned glad to have got rid of you!" he concluded.

The boy also regarded the street. He thought of his aunt's small house down the road with its full cargo of children and adults. He thought of his narrow bed there, pushed into a corner with his bundle of possessions on it. He thought of the long journey by foot and by bus he had taken to get to the city, to get a job, to get money. And he thought of the hut in the small village, so many miles away, where his family waited hopefully.

"Mr Singh . . . "

Mr Singh lit a cheroot expansively, relaxing with the air of a man who has finally got his affairs in order and looks forward to a settled and prosperous future.

"I am deaf, boy."

"Are you still going to Pole Pole tomorrow, Mr Singh?"

"What has that got to do with you?" Mr Singh raised a hand in salutation to the grocer from the shop next door who was seated in the barber's chair on the opposite pavement watching him stonily while his hair was being cut. The grocer did not respond. In retaliation, Mr Singh turned on the grocer's sons in their Sinatra hats who were now drawing figures on the dusty side panels of Mr Singh's truck and told them to clear off. As he returned to his garage, the soft voice of the boy came back again insistently.

"You are going to get the spare parts for the Rolls Royce?"

"I am."

"Will it be the final parts?"

Mr Singh smiled to himself. "It will. Then it will be finished."

Mr Singh strode round the garage to the small garden at the back. There, under a line of washing, stood his Rolls Royce, and in the front seat sat his two older children pretending to drive it. Mr Singh gave a yelp of annoyance and dashed at them. The children scrambled out and disappeared into the house. Mr Singh wiped a few finger marks off the vehicle.

"Look at that, you yokel, you *bara* boy, and you will understand ambition. Ever since I was a young man I have dreamed of having a Rolls Royce. I could never afford such a thing, but I could build it. Ten years I have been building it. Now it will be finished. That is success. You think about that!"

The boy stood at the end of the garage and looked at Mr Singh's Rolls Royce. He was angry at being called a *bara* boy. But he did not show it.

"Mr Singh, I do not think you can make real Rolls Royce."

"What do you mean?"

"Only a Rolls Royce maker could make a real Rolls Royce. You could make something that looked like a Rolls Royce, but it would not be a Rolls Royce. It would not work."

"I am telling you, boy – "

"Mr Singh, you could not make an elephant, could you?"

"I would not *want* to make an elephant – "

"Only God can make an elephant. Even if you knew all about elephants, and you built an elephant that had tusks and big ears and a trunk – it would not be an elephant. Only an elephant maker can make an elephant. I do not think you can make a Rolls Royce."

"I am telling you, boy, you are an ignorant *bara* boy and you know nothing! All your life you live in a village and you know nothing! Very soon, I will drive my Rolls Royce round this town. It will be Singh's Rolls Royce. *I* will be the maker!"

The boy looked away from Mr Singh and murmured to himself, "Still, it will not work. You cannot make a Rolls Royce. It would not be a Rolls Royce." Then he turned to Mr Singh. "Are you going to look at the Pole Pole Rolls Royce for the spare parts?"

"*The* Pole Pole Rolls Royce! What do you mean, boy? There is a Rolls Royce advertised for spare parts at Pole Pole. I am going to look at it. It is not *the* Pole Pole Rolls Royce! What a fool!"

"Now that I have no job, Mr Singh, I must go back to my village. It is to the west not far from Pole Pole."

"If your village was not far from heaven it would not help you."

Mr Singh strode to the front of the garage, but the boy's voice followed with a soft insistence. "I would not be any trouble. I would sit in the back of the truck. I would not speak the whole time."

Mr Singh opened another bottle of orange squash. "Go by bus."

"I have no money."

"Then walk!"

"It would take so long . . . I would not even move the whole time –"

"No!" shouted Mr Singh, and choked on his drink, sputtering it all down his dungarees.

*   *   *

The boy's aunt was sharing out the evening *posho* to the four young children. The boy hesitated, then accepted his share.

"You are going with Mr Singh?" his aunt asked.

"He will not take me."

"He is a mean man! What would it cost him?"

"I think he does not like me."

His aunt ate for a few moments thoughtfully. "Maybe he is right," she concluded, softly. "But that does not help. Are you still wearing your *gethiito*, Kamau? It should help against Mr Singh's hatred."

Kamau touched the charm that was bound to his wrist. He looked dreamily ahead. "Mr Singh does not hate me. He just does not understand me," he said. "But I understand him. That is what makes him angry."

The day darkened, the lights went on in the street. The boy stood in the doorway of his aunt's house, his nephews and nieces playing about his feet. He did not see the street in front of him. He saw himself arriving at his village in Mr Singh's truck. Mr Singh would not, of course, wait, but he would wave to the boy as he left. "That is my boss," he would tell his family. "He has a big garage. He is teaching me to be a mechanic. When I go back to the town, I will work for him again."

"And what he pay for that, man?" his sister would ask sharply.

"Pay? You don't get paid for going to school, do you? Mr Singh spend lots of time teaching me. When I know everything, then I work for him and he pay me a lot of money . . . "

But that was only a dream. He had no money, no job. Mr Singh would never take him back. He had come to the city to find work, but he had no work. He would have to go back to the village of round, thatched huts near the dusty road that took people once a week to the nearby market. He would have to live the monotonous life of the village, obedient to his father, governed by the old tribal superstitions, hemmed in by village gossip. No freedom, no excitement, no chance to get a job and be independent – but he could not stay in the city to live on his aunt.

Further down the street was Mr Singh's truck. Mr Singh was checking the oil and water, ready for the journey next day. His wife stood watching, a cardigan over her sari, the baby on her arm. She pointed out to Mr Singh that one of his tyres was flat and Mr Singh swore angrily and ran into the garage.

When he came out, the boy was standing by the truck. "Mr Singh, I know where there is a Rolls Royce with many good parts. If you will take me with you, I can get it for you."

Mr Singh glared at the boy. Then he burst out laughing. He laughed so loudly, his wife stared in alarm.

"It is true, Mr Singh. It is not joke," said the boy earnestly.

Suddenly Mr Singh stopped laughing. He pointed a long finger at the boy. "You! An ignorant *bara* boy who cannot hold down a job – you know where there is a Rolls Royce and you can get it for me! Go away, boy! Away!"

The boy retreated a few yards. Dreamily he watched Mr Singh changing the tyre. He thought of his grandmother and her prophecy that he would be a successful man, a credit to his family and his people. He was to be the clever one. Now he would have to go back to his village, a failure. Slowly an idea formed in his mind. I will come back here, he said to himself. I will not stay in the village. I will come back. Mr Singh will bring me back.

Mr Singh did not know what he was thinking and so his peace of mind on that score was not disturbed.

*   *   *

In the cool of the early morning, Mr Singh appeared outside the garage, ready for the journey. Carefully he stowed away in the cab of the truck the tin of curry his wife had prepared and several bottles of orange squash. Carefully he checked that the tarpaulin on the back of the truck was secure. He sanguinely kicked each tyre, just to make sure. His wife watched him from the garage doorway, expressionless, baby on arm.

Mr Singh was about to get into the truck when a thought struck him. He returned to his wife. "That Kikuyu boy from along the street – don't let him near this place. Keep the garage locked, don't go out, and don't let him near. Otherwise he is likely to burn it down or blow it up or . . ." Ideas failed him. "I will be gone only a day," he concluded, and got into the truck.

The engine roared in the quiet street.

"And keep those kids off my Rolls Royce!" shouted Mr Singh.

His arm from the truck window waved a farewell to his wife. Her arm was raised in return, the sari falling away behind her shoulder.

It was then that the tarpaulin over the back of the lorry was raised six inches and the large, dark eyes of the boy peered out at Mr Singh's wife. She saw the boy. In sudden anxiety, she stepped forward, waving her arm, shouting, "The boy – he is in the back of the truck!"

Mr Singh saw her through the driving mirror. He shrugged. What a fuss she was making. Just saying goodbye. She was too excitable. He'd always thought so. He should have married her sister instead. But it was too late now! Once again his arm waved from the window, and then the truck accelerated fast out of the city.

And from under the tarpaulin the boy's eyes watched as the streets drew away behind them.

Chapter Two

MR Singh was a flamboyant and erratic driver. Crouched over the wheel with a face of malevolent ferocity, he would take bumpy laterite roads at enormous speed. His truck with its horn blaring scattered herds of goats into a panic, froze innocent pedestrians and unsuspecting drivers into attitudes of horror. But he would, on a good stretch of fast road, suddenly sit back and take his ease, slowing almost to walking pace, well out in the middle of the road, one arm out of the window clasping the hot roof of the truck, his dreaming face totally unaware of the indignation of the drivers he was holding up in a frustrated queue behind him.

He was, therefore, constantly surprised on that journey when he saw, from his driving mirror, people he had just scraped past waving at him, and even women stooped with heavy bundles raising their eyes to smile at his retreat.

He did not know that in the back of the truck, with the tarpaulin thrown back, Kamau squatted, gripping the tail-board with one hand and waving and smiling triumphantly to everyone they passed. The boy was happier now. At least he was getting nearer and nearer to his home. With a bit of luck he might even pick up some money on the way so that his family would be thankful to see him.

Mr Singh was in one of his dreaming moods when they reached the top of the escarpment above the Great Rift Valley with its wide, flat bottom and chain of lakes and extinct volcanoes. The road clung like a cobweb round the escarpment, and Mr Singh began the steep winding descent without thought. When he came to, the truck was coasting at an alarming rate round several hairpin bends. Mr Singh sat up, gripped the wheel fiercely and with wild eyes tried to keep the vehicle on the road, his horn at full blast. At the bottom, suddenly glimpsing a sign post, he took a sharp turn on to a minor road and rattled along for several miles, coming to a sudden stop in the centre of Pole Pole.

"I will never get used to this bloody country," he muttered, as he got out and glared round at the surprised passers-by. "Now where is this damned Rolls Royce?"

He stood looking up and down the street. He had not been there before, but an advertisement in the newspaper had suggested that the spare parts were to be had here at a ridiculously low price at The Best Prices Scrap-Yard.

Mr Singh was suddenly approached by a smart individual in uniform who stepped up to him and saluted.

"Good morning, sir. Follow me," said the stranger.

Mr Singh was startled. "What's that?"

"Follow me."

"You know where this Best Prices Scrap-Yard is?"

"Follow me, sir. Good morning."

Mr Singh hesitated. He scratched his nose. But then he began to follow the man in the uniform with the military bearing along the street.

"Mr Singh!"

Mr Singh whirled round. He stared at the boy who was just behind him.

"My God! How did you get here? Where am I?"

"Mr Singh, do not follow that man."

"You must be your brother – your twin brother!"

"Mr Singh, that man, he is – "

"You can't be your brother – how did you get here?"

"Good morning, sir. Follow me," said the stranger, who had paused with Mr Singh.

"I came in the truck – Mr Singh . . . "

"You stole a lift in my truck!"

"Mr Singh, I know this town – I know that man. This town is bewitched. Please do not follow him . . . "

"Follow me, sir."

"This gentleman is a town official. Why else is he in uniform? He is taking me to Best Prices Scrap-Yard. When I come back you had better not be here or I will ask this official to put you in jail!" Mr Singh went off after the man in uniform. The man saluted people at intervals. Mr Singh's back straightened. He marched in the man's shadow.

They disappeared round the corner. "I will guard this truck, Mr Singh," shouted he boy. Kamau went back and leant on the bonnet. His dark eyes looked sadly up and down the street. "He will come back," he said. "He should have listened to me, even if I *am* only a *bara* boy."

A very old man, leaning on a long staff, halted beside the boy.

"What news, boy?"

"Good news, *mzee*."

"You are a traveller?"

"I am returning to my village."

"Is it to the west?"

"It is."

"Is this your truck?"

"It is the truck of my friend."

"Perhaps I could travel with you? I am an old man and I am tired of walking."

The boy hesitated. "My friend," he said, "is a generous man. But he might not like to give a lift to a stranger. But if you get under the tarpaulin and he doesn't see you, he will not object."

"A few miles along the road even would help," said the old man, and clambered on to the truck.

"Where is your friend?"

"He is looking for the Best Prices Scrap-Yard."

"Does he not know this town is bewitched?"

"Mr Singh does not find it easy to listen to me. But he is a man of great hope. He is building his own Rolls Royce."

"What is that?"

"It is a large car. Like an elephant."

"That is a strange thing for a man to be doing. Building a car like an elephant. Will it have ears and tusks?"

"No, no. It is not like that. It is like . . . " The boy shrugged. He looked down the street for a sign of Mr Singh.

"I told him," he said, "that he would not be able to build a Rolls Royce. Not a real one."

*   *   *

An hour later, Mr Singh, very hot and angry, suddenly appeared before the boy who was sitting on the curb by the truck.

Mr Singh said nothing. He only glared.

19

"Mr Singh, I told you about that man – "

"His is mad! *Mad!* I have followed him everywhere – all over this bloody town! He salutes and salutes and says 'Follow me' – but he does not take me anywhere! Three times I have been round this town!"

"I tried to tell you," said the boy. "He is a poor man and the sun got into his brain. But he does no harm."

"No harm!" No harm to *you* – but I have walked round this town like a fool for one hour! One hour! And no bloody scrap-yard!"

"Mr Singh. I would like to tell you something else."

"I do not want to hear!"

"It will help you."

"You have never yet helped me. If it hadn't been for you, maybe I would never have met that mad man."

"I tried to tell you, Mr Singh."

Mr Singh looked thoughtful. Then he looked suspicious. "What is it?"

"I know where Best Prices Scrap-Yard is."

"You *know*? You *know* and do not tell me? You let me wander around – "

"Mr Singh, whenever I try to tell you, you will not listen. I take you there now."

The scrap-yard was a small wooden hut with a shaky verandah and a dusty compound behind it in which, among scratching hens, a man and a fat woman sat in chairs under a tree. Above the door was a faded notice: BEST PRICES SCRAP-YARD.

Mr Singh looked at this in despair. "This is it?"

The boy nodded.

"The Rolls Royce is here?"

The boy shrugged. "*The* Pole Pole Rolls Royce is here."

"You keep on saying *the* Pole Pole Rolls Royce – where is it? I cannot see it."

There was only one vehicle in sight. A rusting Morris without wheels that had settled like an old elephant waiting for death in a corner of the compound.

"That is the Pole Pole Rolls Royce, Mr Singh."

Mr Singh strode into the compound and up to the man in the chair. The man looked at him with eyes that were full of dreams and did not see Mr Singh or the boy.

"I am Mr Singh from Nairobi," said Mr Singh. "My card."

The man took the card carefully, as though it were a precious jewel. He handled it carefully, reading it, turning it over and nodding his head, then he showed it to his wife. They talked together about it in low voices.

"You put an advertisement in the paper about a Rolls Royce being broken up for spares."

The man stared dreamily at the old Morris and nodded.

"A Rolls Royce," he murmured. "Owned once by important official."

"Where is it?"

The man pointed a lean finger at the Morris. "A very important Rolls Royce," he murmured.

Mr Singh looked aghast, first at the Morris, then at the man, then at the boy.

"He is mad?" he muttered.

"He has had a spell put on his eyes by an enemy. He does not see this world as it is, now. Only as he would like it to be."

Mr Singh shrugged his shoulders in despair and strode out of the compound. Then he stood in the roadway, raised his arms and gave a wild wail.

"Mr Singh!"

"What!"

"I try to tell you this town was bewitched by a bad magician many years ago. So people here are very strange. Everybody knows this. Everybody knows about the Pole Pole Rolls Royce."

"Everybody knows? I did not know! I will never get used to this bloody country!" And Mr Singh stamped along the street, waving his arms at the high, serene African sky.

"Please do not explode again. I tried to tell you all this."

Mr Singh whirled round at him. "And why should I listen to you? A *bara* boy!"

"Because I was right, Mr Singh. But you are not very good at listening to anybody," he added.

Mr Singh drooped under his troubles. "I have come miles – in answer to the advertisement!"

"Do not explode, please," the boy repeated.

Mr Singh looked at the boy. "No. I will not explode. I will despair. And I will go home. Waste of time and petrol! And *you* will stay here!"

The boy's eyes narrowed with worry as he watched Mr Singh stride away along the street, occasionally shaking an irate fist at the sky and brushing away a street vendor who tried to sell him a hand-made pot.

Stay here? He couldn't stay here! He knew nobody in that town – he couldn't be left here! He rushed after Mr Singh.

"Mr Singh," he said earnestly. "I can get Rolls Royce spare parts. I told you this. I know where there are many. Very cheap!"

"How can *you* know – "

"I know. I can show you."

They looked into each other's eyes, Mr Singh's narrowed and suspicious, the boy's wide and anxious.

"How far?"

"A few miles. To the west."

"What is a few?"

"A few."

"What is the place called?"

"Kora."

"Kora?" Mr Singh was suspicious. The name meant "Where the road runs out".

Kamau nodded.

"Draw me a plan . . . " Mr Singh began to feel in his pockets for pencil and paper, but the boy picked up a stick from the roadside and began to sketch in the dust.

"See – this is Pole Pole, where we are. That is the road we came in on. You take that road out in the other direction. You pass a lake, you get to Kora, you pass Kora Clean Hotel, you pass one large fig tree, the turning to one village, then there is a turning which leads to where the Rolls Royce is!"

Mr Singh studied the map with wrinkled brow. "This is bloody uncivilised," he muttered. "Drawing with sticks in dirt . . . one fig tree, one turning to village! My God!" He marched to his truck.

"Please, Mr Singh, take me with you!"

Mr Singh turned in a rage. "Did you drain the radiator of that Ford Cortina?" He thumped the roof of the truck. "Did you break that new bloody jack?" He thumped the roof again. "Did you spray paint on Mr Manani's – chief-clerk-at-Kabete-stores – windscreen?" And he thumped the roof again. "Did you reverse that car of Mr Ruben's into the lamp-post?" He thumped the roof again. "What else have you done? I cannot bear to remember! I am not taking *you*!"

And he leapt into the truck and drove off. The boy stood watching in dismay, and the old man on the truck sat watching him, with mild, unconcerned eyes. Then the truck stopped at the traffic lights. The boy burst into a swift sprint, and leapt on to the back of the truck just as it started again.

"We are going to the west," he panted to the old man.

The old man nodded. "Good. That is to my home."

Chapter Three

THEY drove along the verge of a lake whose still waters glinted like steel in the sun. An old tree raised its dead grey arms from the lake to the sky, with a single fish eagle perched there as still as a stone. A flurry of flamingoes rose in a pink cloud. Beyond the open fish market by the roadside, beyond the lake, a herd of giraffes watched the truck go past, like large-eyed, dreaming visionaries.

Near a small group of trees Mr Singh stopped his truck, making sure it was in the shade. He got out, stretched, glanced at his watch, then took the tin of curry out of the truck. Singing quietly to himself he disappeared among the trees to eat the curry.

The boy and the old man cautiously lifted the tarpaulin and looked out.

"We have not so far to go now, *mzee*," Kamau said.

"What happened to your friend in the bewitched town?" asked the old man.

"He got very angry. He gets angry very quickly. And he does not listen."

"Does he not understand about bewitchment? You should get him a spell to protect him from such dangers."

"He would not have it. His religion is different. He believes only in cars, I think. And spare parts."

A woman bent double under a bundle of firewood walked up to the truck. "Are you going to the west?" she asked.

"We are."

"Will you take me? This bundle is very heavy."

The boy hesitated. Then he shrugged. "Why not? If Mr Singh objects to me and to the old father here, he might as well object to you."

And he helped the woman on to the truck with her bundle.

"Are you going to your village or away from your village?" she asked. She smiled as she asked. She smiled all the time.

"I am going to my village, but my friend who owns this truck is going away from his. He is looking for spare parts."

The woman smiled. "Spare parts? What is spare parts?"

"The owner of this truck," said the old man, "is fiery as the sun and proud as a Masai. He believes he can build a motor car that looks like an elephant."

The woman giggled.

"No, no," said the boy, his brow furrowed, "that is not it. My friend is building a large motor car, a car as big as an *elephant*."

"That is equally impossible," said the old man. "How would he get on to its back?"

"It will have doors, and a step."

"It will be like the hotel in Pole Pole!" cried the woman, laughing.

The old man smiled and the boy laughed also. "With big windows!"

"And a garden!"

"And tables and chairs . . . "

They were doubled up with laughter, when they heard Mr Singh returning, and hastily pulled down the tarpaulin.

Mr Singh returned refreshed to his truck and drove off again towards the west. This time he drove more slowly, watching the road dreamily and singing a mournful Indian song under his breath.

At Kora, he again parked the truck and strode off to find a scrap-yard. The boy, the old man and the woman got out of the truck to stretch their legs. They bought bottles of soft drinks, for it was hot travelling on the back of the truck, and they sat on the truck to drink them.

Two Masai youths, tall and lean in their red cloaks, strode up to the truck and climbed on.

Kamau was dismayed. "You cannot do this," he said. "This is not a public vehicle. It belongs to my friend, Mr Singh."

"You are going to the west?" the tallest Masai asked.

Kamau nodded. "Yes, but – "

"Good. We come with you."

Kamau looked at them. One was about his own age, his hair short and unbraided. But the other was older, his hair was plaited, and he carried a spear. He was a warrior and had proved himself. It would not be easy to throw him off the truck. In fact, it would be impossible.

Kamau accepted the inevitable.

"We are not going very far," he warned them. "But I will let you travel that distance with us."

The Masai, gazing before them as though over vast distances of grazing land, appeared not to hear him.

"This boy's friend, Mr Singh," said the old man, "is building a car like an elephant."

"No, no," protested Kamau. "As big as an elephant. It began when he was only a child. Sleeping in his hut one night, God spoke to him in a dream and said, 'Mr Singh, you must build a Rolls Royce like an elephant.' And when he wakened he made a vow that when he grew up he would buy pieces of Rolls Royce and build a car. Mr Singh has kept his vow. He is building a Rolls Royce. Only, it will not be a real Rolls Royce."

"Does your friend have a lot of cattle? Is he rich?"

"No, he has no cattle . . . "

"Then he should buy cattle not pieces of cars," said the older Masai, with a scornful and decided look.

"That is not what Mr Singh wants. What use would cattle be to Mr Singh? He could not keep cattle in a street in Nairobi . . . "

They were so involved in the argument that they did not see Mr Singh until he was suddenly beside them, and had seized Kamau by his shirt and dragged him off the truck.

"Who are these people? Why are they on my truck? Get off! Get away from here."

Reluctantly, the woman, the old man and the two Masai climbed down. They stood looking at Mr Singh and the boy.

"You!" cried Mr Singh. "How are you here again? Why are you following me?"

"Mr Singh," stammered the boy, "I am not following you. I am going home, Mr Singh."

"And where are these spare parts in Kora? Nobody knows about them. You lie to me again. You are a walking disaster!"

"Mr Singh, not Kora – *near* Kora. Very near. I showed you on the map – past the fig tree, past the – "

"*Map!* Scribbled in the dust – that was a map!" He fumed silently for a few moments, then grasped Kamau by the shoulder. "Right. I give you last chance. And what last chance means is last bloody chance! You come in the front of the truck and show me!"

Kamau smiled with relief. "And, Mr Singh," he said persuasively, "these people are my friends. It would not hurt you to give them a lift – "

"No!" roared Mr Singh. "Am I running a bus service?" He glared at the small group of people watching with polite interest, revealing none of their anxiety to get a lift. "Get in the truck, boy. And if you don't find these spare parts, I will . . . I will . . . I will take your liver with me back to Nairobi!"

The small group murmured with shock and moved back a little. Kamau searched Mr Singh's face, anxiously.

"But, Mr Singh . . . You would not . . . you could not," he stammered. "In any case, I do not think you would like my liver . . . "

"What?" roared Mr Singh. "Do you suggest I am a cannibal?"

Kamau got swiftly into the truck.

As they drove off, he looked back sadly at the little group of people they left. Then his eyes widened in horror. The older Masai boy had raised his spear.

The shaft of the spear rattled against the door beside Mr Singh, while the blade buried itself in the front tyre. Mr Singh put his foot on the brake.

"My God!" he shouted. "We are being attacked!"

Some time later, Mr Singh finished changing the wheel, assisted by the boy and watched by the same small group of people. Irate and oily, he strode away to the Kora Clean Hotel, a three-sided hut with a tin roof, to drink a bottle of orange squash.

As soon as he disappeared, the boy beckoned to the old man, the woman and the two Masai, and lifted the tarpaulin at the back of the truck. As they scrambled on, a girl carrying a large, heavy basket came running up. She was slightly taller than Kamau, lean as a reed, in a crumpled, dirty frock, and it seemed that the heavy basket would pull her over.

"Are you going to the west?" she panted.

"I am going to the west."

"Take me with you. I have missed the bus. I cannot walk home with this basket."

"This is not my truck. It is my friend's truck. He would not like it!"

"But you have so many people already! I am not heavy."

"She would not make much difference," said the old man.

"She will not get home today otherwise," smiled the woman.

The two Masai said nothing.

"Oh, all right!" said Kamau. "Here, give me the basket."

The girl and her basket were squeezed on to the truck. The boy pulled the tarpaulin over them and scrambled into the front seat just as Mr Singh returned, still muttering angrily.

"At least we have got rid of that African rabble!" he said and started the truck with a jerk. They went bouncing along the road out of Kora.

Chapter Four

THEY were travelling now through terraced hills and thickly wooded valleys, and Kamau, knowing he was nearing home, looked out for the glimpses of the white peaks of Mount Kenya that appeared and disappeared with each bend of the road.

"So," said Mr Singh, as they went, "now you are going back to your village. To be a *bara* boy, again, eh? That is where you belong."

"I will not just be a *bara* boy, Mr Singh. You see, when I was born my grandmother prophesied that I would be a very successful business-man. This is why my father sold many goats to get money to send me to the city to find a job."

Mr Singh laughed scornfully. "Not very good at prophesying, your grandmother, eh?"

"Oh yes. She was very good. All her prophecies come true. Also, she gave me this special charm to wear." He touched the charm on his wrist. "It is a charm to keep away bad influences. So I will not be a *bara* boy, Mr Singh."

"Superstitions! You get nowhere on superstitions!"

"But that is not true, Mr Singh. You yourself told me that when you were a young boy you had a dream in your hut in which God spoke to you and said, 'Mr Singh, build a Rolls Royce' and that is what you are doing . . . "

Mr Singh thumped the wheel. "That is not true! I had no dream! I had an ambition! That is different! And I tell you this – if there are no spare parts – I call the police. Too bloody true, I will!"

"There are spare parts. You will see."

"Yes, I will see! and *you* will see what I do if there are not! Do not argue!"

"I am not arguing, Mr Singh. I am only telling the truth. You see, Mr Singh, my father is a doctor. He has supernatural powers. Also, all his forefathers had these powers, so these powers will pass to me . . . "

Mr Singh turned to look at the boy, his eyes wide, fogetting the road. "You – are – a – *bara* boy!"

And suddenly, the boy saw the turning to his village. "Turn left, Mr Singh! Left!"

Mr Singh stopped abruptly, and everyone was thrown forward. He glared at the narrow track to the left. "Down there?"

It led through a deep woodland, narrow and rutted and shaded from the sun.

"How can anything be down there? Boy, you are fooling me again!"

"No, Mr Singh. I tell you truth. Down here we find plenty spare parts."

The truck started again. Mr Singh put it fast down the track. The boy clung to the seat, and on the back the old man, the woman and the two Masai and the girl bounced up and down.

Suddenly, as they rounded a bend, they saw an elephant blocking the way. It was a large elephant, red from a dust bath. Mr Singh screamed the truck to a halt.

The elephant watched the truck with mild curiosity with his small, sly eyes. His face seemed fixed in smile, as if he was laughing inwardly at them.

"My God!" Mr Singh shouted. "I knew it. I knew you would bring more trouble. You are a disaster! A disaster! Bloody elephant." And he put his hand hard on the horn.

The elephant moved one foot restlessly, put his head up, flapped his ears, and waved his trunk.

"Mr Singh, Mr Singh, please don't! Elephants have right of way! Go back. Go back!" Kamau pleaded.

"I will *not* go back! That damned animal can go away."

The elephant lowered his head and trumpeted. Mr Singh's eyes
started – he knew the animal meant business. Hastily, he put the truck
into reverse. But it wouldn't move. The wheels turned and turned in a
rut, digging deeper and deeper.

"Get out! Get out! My God! I'll lose my truck as well. He'll toss it
away!"

"No, no, Mr Singh. Take it out of gear! Take the brake off!"

Kamau leapt out of the truck. "Come on," he shouted to the others.
"Come on! Push the truck! Push it back!"

The passengers spilled out and began to heave at the truck. Mr Singh watched them with fearful and incredulous eyes. At first, the truck wouldn't move, and the elephant, still watching with his inward smile, moved a step forward. Then the truck rolled backwards, Mr Singh thrust it into reverse, and it shot round the corner backwards, with the others running after it. In a quiet glade they stopped, listening breathlessly, to the cracking of branches as the elephant moved ponderously away.

Kamau looked in at Mr Singh. "All right now, Mr Singh?" he smiled. "O.K., eh?"

Mr Singh mopped his brow with a shaking hand. He stared round at them. "My God," he murmured, "what a journey! Load of bloody car squatters! And I only wanted spare parts!"

Beyond the woodland, on a ridge, lay Kamau's village, quiet under the late sun, smoke rising from the cooking fires. Kamau's family's huts clustered together inside a pallisade. The women were still returning from the plantations.

Kamau's mother, busy at the fire, looked up as Mr Singh's truck bucked over the rough earth. His sister looked up from the freshly-brewed beer she was pouring into a gourd and his two younger brothers came to the door of his mother's hut. Outside his father's hut, a group of elders sat, stopping their discussion to examine the visitors.

There was a look of poverty and weariness in the faces of Kamau's parents, and when they saw that their son had returned, there was shock also. They said nothing, but their silence meant everything to Kamau. He saw tears on his mother's face as she turned away, trying to hide her disappointment. They had worked so hard, sold so many goats to get their son to the city, and here he was returning, not in his own car, or even on his own motor bike, but in an old shirt and shorts. Nothing suggested he had been successful.

Kamau climbed down from Mr Singh's truck, and for a moment stood looking at the familiar scene, hesitating, knowing in his heart that the most difficult part of his journey had come. Then he went to receive his parents' blessing on his return.

They gave them to him willingly, but sorrowfully.

"You are welcome home, son," said his father. "Have you brought these friends from the city?"

Kamau tried to appear confident.

"No, no father. My boss, Mr Singh, is a kind man, and gave them a lift."

"That is your boss?" asked his sister. "He has brought you home? Why would he do that?"

Kamau forced himself to smile. "I will tell you everything soon. But first, we must welcome Mr Singh."

"He does not look as though he wants to be welcomed," said Kamau's sister, who was a shrewd girl. Kamau ignored this.

Mr Singh was gazing with some disgust at his passengers as they climbed down and greeted the villagers, and at Kamau and his family.

Kamau's father went to welcome him, and offered him some refreshment, but Kamau stepped forward quickly.

"Please, father. First I have some business to conclude with Mr Singh."

It sounded very impressive to everybody.

"Yes," said Mr Singh, angrily. "Spare parts!"

"Please come this way," said Kamau, leading Mr Singh past his mother's hut.

Beyond the hut, near the pallisade, was a Rolls Royce, rusted, but intact, and standing incongruously against a backdrop of the vast African plains scattered with humped thorn trees, tinged by the sun, and with a strange air of waiting in the eternal, patient silence of the countryside.

"My God!" exclaimed Mr Singh. "It *is* a Rolls Royce! All there! All parts there! Whose is this?"

"It is mine."

"Yours? How can a *bara* boy own a Rolls Royce? It is stolen!"

"How could I steal such a car? Out in the country here? Everybody would know about it. No. It is mine. My family have papers to prove this. When the white man here left, he told my father to take this car. My father had worked for him for a long time. And the white man said he could not take it away with him. My father said to me, 'Son, this kind of thing is not for me. I am not of such a modern age. But you will be when you grow up. So this is yours.'"

"And why did you keep this secret? Why did you not tell me before? You watched me build a Rolls Royce and you did not tell me you had one! You are a bloody *bara* boy! A Tick!"

Kamau regarded him with dignity.

"Mr Singh, why should I tell you when you were happy building your own Rolls Royce? What use would this be to you then? Only when you could not get the spare parts was it useful to you. Then I told you. Before, it was not necessary. And even if I have been a walking disaster to you, Mr Singh, it was not done deliberately. Sometimes I think I had a bad spell put on me by an enemy and that made me unlucky. However, that has passed, as you can see. If I had not given these people a lift on your truck, Mr Singh, your truck would now be dismantled in the forest there by the elephant. Also, if I had not had this Rolls Royce, you would be without spare parts."

Mr Singh looked crafty. "Maybe. But it is no use to you, of course. You cannot drive it. You have no money for petrol – "

"Engine still works," said Kamau, and went to switch it on. After a few coughs, it started, shaking the whole vehicle. "I have looked after it."

"All right, all right. How much do you want?"

"For spare parts or whole thing?"

"Maybe for whole thing – maybe not."

"It would be a pity to break up such a fine vehicle. A man like you could work on it – drive it away – altogether!"

"How much?"

"Mr Singh." The boy's dark eyes held his. "I make bargain. For maybe one thousand shillings and one other consideration you can have Rolls Royce."

Mr Singh gave a skip of ecstasy and then stopped.

"What consideration?"

The boy hesitated. Then he said, "You take me back – give me job again, also pay wages."

Mr Singh gave a howl, like a hyena at night, and raised his fists to heaven.

"Mr Singh," said the boy quickly, "please do not explode. Only in that way can you have this car. One thousand shillings I can give to my

46

parents as money I have earned. Also, I can say to my parents I have good job in Nairobi."

Mr Singh howled again. He went to the Rolls and stroked its bonnet gently, then he turned and walked quickly away shaking his head. Then he came back and glared at Kamau.

"All right. A bargain. But the first time you do something disastrous – "

"I will be careful. Also, Mr Singh, your dream has come to pass."

"What dream?"

"The dream that began it. When you lay in your hut and God came to you and said, 'Mr Singh, make a car as big as an elephant.'"

Mr Singh's eyes opened wide. "What are you talking about? What hut? What dream? . . ."

Hastily Kamau changed the subject. "Come, Mr Singh. Come to my father's hut and have some beer . . . When you are ready you can come back here and take the Rolls Royce away."

"I must get a lorry," said Mr Singh. "I must tow it to Nairobi. It will be Singh's Rolls Royce . . . " He went on chattering as Kamau led him back to the huts.

It was later, when the western sky was red with the sunset and night falling on the village, that Kamau and Mr Singh began their journey back to Nairobi.

As the truck moved slowly away, the village children trailed after them, singing:

Kamau's boss built a car – wooee!
Big as an elephant – wooee!
He is taking Kamau back to the city with him.

And Kamau leaned out, waving and singing:
Kamau will be a rich man –

And the children sang:
Who knows how rich he will be?
Woee! Woee!

And Mr Singh, clutching the wheel, and frowning fiercely, muttered, "Bloody *bara* boy! Walking disaster!"